For Karen Klingon, my sister in spirit,
with thanks to First Lady Michelle Obama
—J.D.

For Amos, Owen, and Margo
—L.G.

The illustrations for this book were made with pencil, ink,
and digital coloring.

Cataloging-in-Publication Data has been applied for and may
be obtained from the Library of Congress.

ISBN 978-1-4197-5246-9

Text © 2022 Jarrett Dapier
Illustrations © 2022 Lee Gatlin
Book design by Jade Rector

Printed and bound in China
10 9 8 7 6 5 4 3 2 1

Abrams® is a registered trademark of Harry N. Abrams, Inc.

ABRAMS The Art of Books
195 Broadway, New York, NY 10007
abramsbooks.com

THE MOST
HAUNTED HOUSE
IN AMERICA

By **Jarrett Dapier**

Illustrated by **Lee Gatlin**

Abrams Books for Young Readers
New York

It was late October, the moon was pale,
late in October when it came by mail:
a letter, a missive, a kind invitation
to drum at

THE MOST HAUNTED HOUSE IN THE NATION!

The First Lady of the United States of America
requests the musical services of
THE SKELETON DRUMMERS

at a Halloween celebration

on October 31st
at
the White House, North Lawn
1600 Pennsylvania Ave.
Washington, D.C., 20500

Be there or be scared.

The White House, the White House,
you've heard of the place:
the First Couple's home, the president's base.
But there's one more thing you might not know:
The White House is **HAUNTED** from top to toe!

We're a little bit nervous, a little bit scared,
but the Skeleton Drummers are always prepared.

So come along, join us, as we make our way
to America's capital, where we'll play.

WASHINGTON, D.C.

We rise from the earth and we CLACK our bones,
climb on the cart and tap double stroke tones.
A drum rig contraption of metal and tin—
perfectly built for a Halloween din.

We skeletons **BOOM!** We skeletons **BANG!**
Brake drums and cymbals and metal go **CLANG!**
We blast beats on buckets and one big old gong—
children in costumes are drawn to our song.

Wizards and witches and robots and more
line up the drive and step up to the door.
Thousands of children, their dads, and their moms
dance to the beat as we thrash on the toms.

Ghost notes, a rim click, then **RATA-MA-CUE!**
Our bass drum makes **THUNDER**, a hullabaloo.
The First Couple grins as kids hoist their sacks,
dropping in cookies and candies and snacks.

A **CLINK!** and a **SHAKE!** in the dim, haunted gloom,
we skeletons **ROCK** the president's home.
Thousand-pound pumpkins aglow in the gloom,
we howl as we drum—a soundtrack of **DOOM!**

Then when the trick-or-treating is through,
the First Couple leads our skeleton crew
into the house, where the dream party moves
to celebrate more to the sound of our grooves.

But inside the doors, something's not right.
A chill in the air and a prickle of fright
grab hold of our band: Our sticks start to **SHAKE**
our bones start to **SHUDDER**,
then **RATTLE**
and **QUAKE!**

We march and we tramp, we strike at our snares.
We're lured by the soft, ghostly music upstairs.
We enter a **RED ROOM** swarming with souls:
They shimmer and sway to our haunted drum rolls.

They twirl and they waltz, they float and they flip.
The lights all go dark, our grip starts to slip.
Two snakes slither by! Let's hope they don't bite!
We back slowly out and keep out of sight.

Back in the hall and more spirits arrive:
They step out of paintings like something **ALIVE!**
Abe Lincoln appears in his stovepipe hat,
scratching the chin of a giant-sized cat.

A **KNOCK!** at the door rings in the wings.
A one-legged rooster hops in and sings:
"Beware of this place, you shouldn't have come!"
A barn owl swoops, its wings beat a **THRUM.**

A **KNOCK!** again at the door down below—
we drum and pretend it's just part of the show.
We're not scared a bit! That raccoon's a fake!
Everything's fine! Try some of the cake!

A violin **SHRIEKS!** in the attic above.
We trip and we bump
and we turn and we shove.
We knock our thick skulls,
we sprint and we fall,

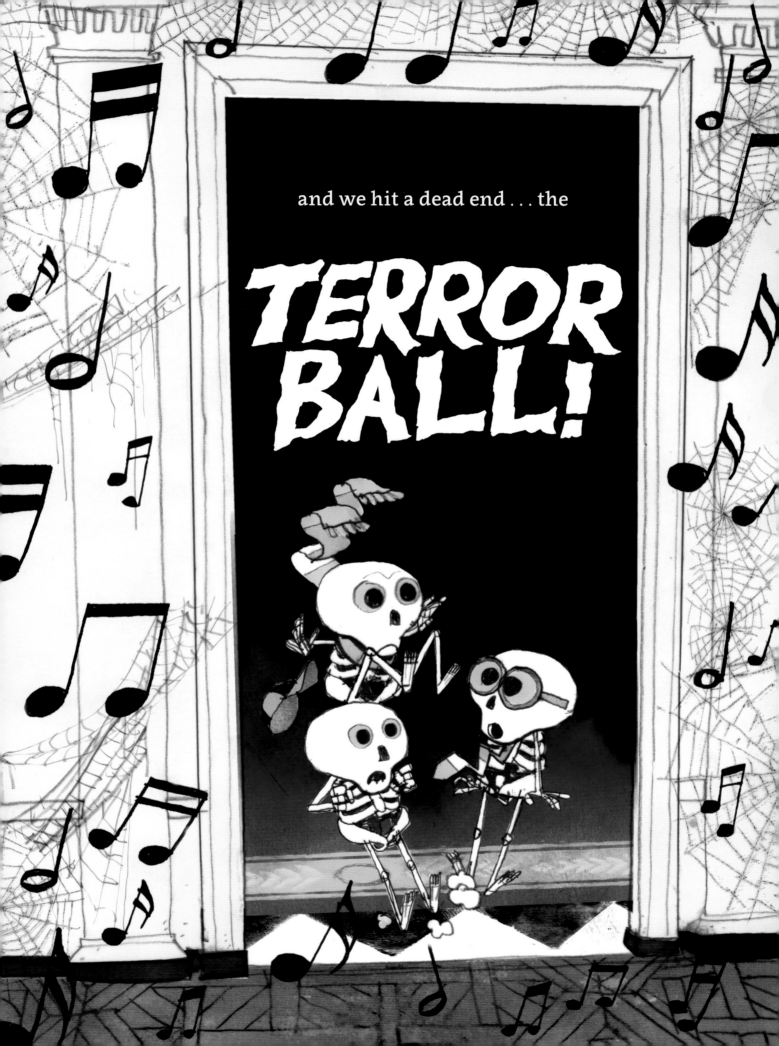

The dead and the living, together at last!
Figures appear right out of the past:
Abigail Adams, Abe Lincoln's son,
a freak called **THE THING—**

EVERYONE RUN!

We flee through the gates out into the dark—
with howls and yelps, we stomp through the park.
We haunt the Mall with our rhythms all night.
Skeleton drummers! A melee of **FRIGHT!**

We creatures all revel and drum till the dawn,
then wearily creep back into the lawn,
climbing deep underground for a whole year to rest.
Thank you, First Lady—this night was the **BEST!**

AUTHOR'S NOTE

The White House is considered by some historians and ghost experts to be the most haunted house in America. This is due to the sheer number of consistently reported and verified ghost sightings that have occurred there for more than a century. The most common ghost that White House visitors and residents have seen is Abraham Lincoln. Presidents, overnight visitors, and White House staffs have seen Old Abe walking down the halls of the living quarters, staring thoughtfully out the window of the Yellow Oval Room (which was his office and library when he was president), and knocking on bedroom doors late at night. Other White House phantoms include First Lady Abigail Adams, the wife of America's second president John Adams, who has been seen hanging laundry in the East Room; First Lady Dolley Madison tending flowers in the famed Rose Garden; Willie Lincoln, President Lincoln's eleven-year-old son, who died in the White House; President Thomas Jefferson playing his violin; and President Andrew Jackson has been heard muttering swear words, which he liked to do when he was angry.

There's more! The Red Room, used as a parlor and dining room by many presidents, was the room where Mary Todd Lincoln once held a séance to contact her deceased son. Guests have reported hearing old 1920s music coming from one of the twenty-eight fireplaces in the house. President Ronald Reagan's dog, Rex, supposedly refused to enter the Lincoln Bedroom and would sit in the doorway barking incessantly at something—or some*one*—in the room that no one else could see. President Roosevelt's dog, Fala, acted similarly. Maybe the dogs both saw the Demon Cat, a tabby cat that supposedly haunts Washington, D.C.'s buildings and grows to the size of an elephant when seen. Or maybe they saw the ghost of one of the past presidents' pets, like Teddy Roosevelt's one-legged rooster, barn owl, or snakes; Calvin Coolidge's raccoon, Rebecca; or Herbert Hoover's alligators!

Perhaps the most mysterious paranormal sighting at the White House was that of a ghost that White House staff named "the Thing." This was the ghost of a fifteen-year-old boy who roamed the halls, frightening White House staff during President William Taft's administration in the early 1900s. So many members of his staff spoke of their startling run-ins with the Thing that President Taft forbade anyone from talking about the ghost. President Taft insisted the Thing didn't exist, but letters unearthed by a historian revealed that the president didn't want anyone talking about the Thing because he was scared of the ghost, too! The Thing was reportedly a teen boy, not the giant eyeball covered in eyeballs we have pictured here, but who's to say the Thing wasn't a shapeshifter?

In 2009, I was invited to play the drums at the White House during the Obamas' first Halloween celebration. Dressed up like a skeleton from top to toe, I jammed away with two other drummer buddies for over two hours straight on the North Lawn, while more than 2,500 children and their favorite grown-ups trick-or-treated at the White House's front door. We performed on a strange, unwieldy drum cart that looked a little bit like a steamroller hung with old oil cans, enormous bass drums, and junky tom-toms, as well as one giant gong that made a huge, gushing sound when we hit it: bbbbbbBBBBWWWAAAAAAASSHHHHHHHHhhhh!!!

I don't *think* I saw any ghosts the night I played at the White House, but who's to say for sure? There were so many people of all sizes and shapes in elaborate costumes both realistic and fantastical, so many enchanting decorations, and so many activities occurring all at once. Maybe the *real* Abraham Lincoln and other ghosts from the past were there, too, watching, dancing, and whispering into our ears as we passed by. Only the ghosts truly know.

Sincerely,
Jarrett Dapier

Tripplaar Kristoffer/sipa/UPI/Shutterstock

Look, there's Jarrett!

For more information on White House ghosts and hauntings in Washington, D.C., check out these other books and online articles:

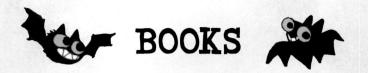 BOOKS

DuMont, Brianna. *Weird But True Know-It-All: U.S. Presidents*. Washington, D.C.: National Geographic Kids, 2017.

Flynn, Sarah Wassner. *1,000 Facts About the White House*. Washington, D.C.: National Geographic Kids, 2017.

Ogden, Tom. *Haunted Washington, D.C.: Federal Phantoms, Government Ghosts, and Beltway Banshees*. Guilford, CT: Globe Pequot, 2016.

 ONLINE

Bushong, William. "Forgotten Ghosts of the White House." *White House Historical Association*, October 19, 2015. See whitehousehistory.org/the-forgotten-ghosts-that-haunted-the-white-house.

Conradt, Stacy. "12 People Who Have Supposedly Seen or Felt Lincoln's Ghost." *Mental Floss*, October 29, 2016. See mentalfloss.com/article/88007/12-people-who-have-supposedly-seen-or-felt-lincolns-ghost.

Ferro, Shaunacy. "'The Thing': The Mysterious Teenage Ghost That Haunted Taft's White House." *Mental Floss*, October 2, 2017. See mentalfloss.com/article/504800/thing-mysterious-teenage-ghost-haunted-tafts-white-house.

Vargas, Theresa. "Is the White House haunted? A history of spooked presidents, prime ministers, and pets." *Washington Post*, October 30, 2017. See washingtonpost.com/news/retropolis/wp/2017/10/30/is-the-white-house-haunted-a-history-of-spooked-presidents-prime-ministers-and-pets.